A Note to Parents

Reading books aloud and playing word games are two valuable ways parents can help their children learn to read. The easy-to-read stories in the **My First Hello Reader! With Flash Cards** series are designed to be enjoyed together. Six activity pages and 16 flash cards in each book help reinforce phonics, sight vocabulary, reading comprehension, and facility with language. Here are some ideas to develop your youngster's reading skills:

Reading with Your Child

- Read the story aloud to your child and look at the colorful illustrations together. Talk about the characters, setting, action, and descriptions. Help your child link the story to events in his or her own life.
- Read parts of the story and invite your child to fill in the missing parts. At first, pause to let your child "read" important last words in a line. Gradually, let your child supply more and more words or phrases. Then take turns reading every other line until your child can read the book independently.

Enjoying the Activity Pages

- Treat each activity as a game to be played for fun. Allow plenty of time to play.
- Read the introductory information aloud and make sure your child understands the directions.

Using the Flash Cards

- Read the words aloud with your child. Talk about the letters and sounds and meanings.
- Match the words on the flash cards with the words in the story.
- Help your child find words that begin with the same letter and sound, words that rhyme, and words with the same ending sound.
- Challenge your child to put flash cards together to make sentences from the story and create new sentences.

Above all else, make reading time together a fun time. Show your child that reading is a pleasant and meaningful activity. Be generous with your praise and know that, as your child's first and most important teacher, you are contributing immensely to his or her command of the printed word.

—Tina Thoburn, Ed.D.
Educational Consultant

For my parents
—K.H.

Copyright © 1996 by Nancy Hall, Inc.
All rights reserved. Published by Scholastic Inc.
MY FIRST HELLO READER!, CARTWHEEL BOOKS, and the
CARTWHEEL BOOKS logo are registered trademarks of Scholastic Inc.
The MY FIRST HELLO READER! logo is a trademark of Scholastic Inc.

Library of Congress Cataloging-in-Publication Data

Hall, Kirsten.
Our tea party / by Kirsten Hall; illustrated by Dee deRosa.
p.   cm. — (My first hello reader!)
"With flash cards!"
"Cartwheel books."
"Preschool - grade 1" — Cover.
"Ages 3-6" — Cover.
Summary: A little girl ignores the snickering of her older brother and his friend as she arranges a tea party for her dog and teddy bear, and eventually the boys find a reason to join the party.
ISBN 0-590-68996-7
[1. Parties — Fiction. 2. Dogs — Fiction. 3. Brothers and sisters — Fiction.]
I. DeRosa, Dee, ill. II. Title. III. Series.
PZ7.H14570u   1996
[E] — dc20

95-51385
CIP
AC

12 11 10 9 8 7 6 5 4 3 2 1   6 7 8 9/9 0 1/0

Printed in the U.S.A.

First Scholastic printing, November 1996

OUR TEA PARTY

by Kirsten Hall
Illustrated by Dee deRosa

My First Hello Reader!
With Flash Cards

SCHOLASTIC INC.
New York   Toronto   London   Auckland   Sydney

Oh, what fun today will be!

We will have a tea party.

Here is a cup . . . a saucer, too.

Some tea for me!

Some tea for you!

Here is some honey.

Doggy
Treat
Biscuits

Here is a spoon.

Our cookies will be ready soon!

Some tea and cookies!

Join the fun!

A tea party for everyone!

Looking On

How do the boys act while the girl is preparing the tea party?

How do the boys act at the end of the story?

Rhyming Words

Match each word on the left to a picture on the right that shows a rhyming word.

tea

spoon

honey

fun

Tea Party Time

Point to the things you might find at a tea party.
Now point to the things that you would not find at a
tea party.

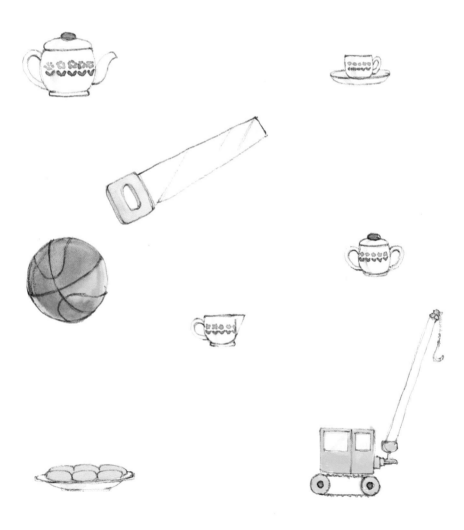

What Do You Think?

Which things could really happen? Which are make-believe?

The boy eats a cookie.

The teddy bear eats some honey.

The girl gets out of bed in the morning.

The dog picks up a teacup in its paw.

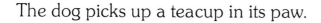

Tasty Treats

Find something sweet and crunchy.

Find something sour.

Find something sweet and sticky.

Find something salty.

Find something wet and hot.

Time for Tea

If you were planning a tea party...

Who would you invite?

Where would your guests sit?

What would you serve your guests to eat and drink?

Who would clean up when the party was over?

Answers

(*Looking On*)

Answers will vary.

(*Rhyming Words*)

tea

spoon

honey

fun

(*Tea Party Time*)

You might find:

You would not find:

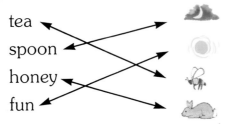

(*What Do You Think?*)

These could really happen:

The boy eats a cookie.
The girl gets out of bed in the morning.

These are make-believe:

The teddy bear eats some honey.
The dog picks up a teacup in its paw.

(*Tasty Treats*)

 are sweet and crunchy.

 is sour.

 is sweet and sticky.

 are salty.

 is wet and hot.